Will Fox Ever Learn?

written by Manny Chiang

illustrated by Tim Egan

McGraw-Hill
School Division

New York   Farmington

Rabbit was alone at home when he heard the
knock at his door. It was Fox.

"Mr. Fox, how marvelous to see you," said
Rabbit. Of course, it wasn't really marvelous to
see Fox—Fox had been trying to catch and eat
Rabbit for years. Rabbit was sick of it.

"Good morning, Rabbit," said Fox. "I was
hoping you might walk with me to the town picnic.
It's a beautiful day, and you shouldn't stay locked
up inside."

"The town picnic—what a splendid idea," said
Rabbit from behind the door. "Unfortunately, though, I
don't feel well enough today to walk to town."

"Well, how about if I give you a ride on my back
then?" asked Fox slyly.

"A ride on your back?" asked Rabbit in
amazement. "No, I might fall off and get hurt. I can
only ride with a saddle."

The sound of Rabbit's voice made Fox's mouth
water. "Okay," Fox agreed and asked Rabbit where
he kept his saddle.

Rabbit watched from the window as Fox saddled himself. "Make it tight," Rabbit called, "and put on the bridle and blinders, too."

"This bridle hurts my mouth," Fox mumbled, "and I can hardly see with these blinders on."

"Good!" thought Rabbit, chuckling to himself. "We're going to make some scene!"

Fox wasn't happy trotting down the road with Rabbit on his back. "I hope nobody sees me," he thought. "If people knew that I let Rabbit ride on my back, I'd be laughed out of town. 'Some predator,' the other animals would say—my reputation would be destroyed."

"Beautiful day for a ride!" commented Rabbit.

"Enjoy it while you can," thought Fox, "because as soon as I get up to those trees, it's going to be a beautiful day for my lunch!"

Rabbit knew what Fox was planning. That's why he had a wooden stake under his jacket. Fox was wearing blinders, so he didn't see Rabbit remove the stake.

At the trees, Fox stopped short. "Okay, Rabbit, the ride's over," he growled. "It's lunch time!"

"Oh, no, it's not," said Rabbit, poking Fox hard with the stake. "Giddy-yap!"

"Eeyoowww!!" roared Fox, leaping into the air and racing down the road. Whenever Fox tried to slow down, Rabbit poked him again.

Fox ran so fast that soon they reached the town picnic.

Turkey, Chicken, and the other fowl saw Fox first. They pointed their wings and laughed and clucked.

Opossum was there with her five daughters. The eldest one giggled behind her paw to see them pass by. Then the younger ones laughed until they rolled in the dirt.

Rat and Skunk sneered at Fox, and Raccoon slapped Turtle on the shell. A bunch of bluejays whistled rudely.

Just then, Fox's blinders came loose. Blinking and looking around, Fox saw the whole town laughing at him! What a mess!

Fox stopped short and stood up on his hind legs. Rabbit lost his grip and went flying.

Rabbit knew his ride was over for good. Holding onto his hat, he made a leap for it, his hind legs sending him flying across the grass.

Fox was on his trail in no time, leaving saddle, bridle, and blinders strewn about behind him.

Fox might have gotten his lunch if Rabbit hadn't seen the hollow tree. There was a hole in one side just big enough for Rabbit to squeeze through.

"You have to come out some time, Rabbit," warned Fox. "When you do, I'll be waiting."

"What's going on?" asked a loud voice. It was Buzzard, who lived at the top of the tree.

"I've got Rabbit trapped in here," answered Fox. "This time, I've got him for sure!"

"It could take a while for Rabbit to come out," said Buzzard. "Why don't you go get your ax, Fox. Then you could chop him out and we could both have a little rabbit for lunch. I'm good and hungry."

"Okay," Fox agreed. "Just don't let him get away! Don't take your eyes off this hole!"

Inside the tree, Rabbit was worried. Fox could chop the hollow tree down in minutes and Buzzard's big claws were just a few inches from Rabbit's nose. What was he going to do?

"Eeeek!" Rabbit screamed. "Eeeek! This tree is full of mice! Don't you ever clean up down here?"

"Mice!" exclaimed Buzzard. His hungry eyes lit up. He wouldn't have minded the chance to clean up a few mice then and there.

"Chase those mice out of the hole," suggested Buzzard. "I'll take care of them."

The tree shook and dust rose as Rabbit supposedly chased those mice. "Git! Git!" he shouted, stamping his feet.

"Buzzard, quick," Rabbit cried, "the mice are getting away! They're escaping out this tiny hole round back!"

Old Buzzard flapped over to the other side of the tree. Sure enough, there was a tiny hole, but he didn't see any mice. He peeked through the hole. Still no mice. All Buzzard saw, in fact, was Rabbit . . . running out the other side of the tree!

A few minutes later, Fox returned, his gleaming ax slung over his shoulder. "You build a fire to cook Rabbit," Fox instructed Buzzard. "I'll chop him out."

Whack! Whack! "It won't be long now, Rabbit," Fox said with a chuckle. When the hole was big enough, Fox stuck his head in.

"I can't see Rabbit anywhere," Fox called out to Buzzard. "You didn't see him get away, did you?"

"Oh, no," Buzzard assured him, tossing more branches onto the fire. "Rabbit's in there somewhere."

Whack! Whack! Soon the hole was big enough for Fox to climb inside.

Fox wasn't in the tree for long. "You let Rabbit escape!" he screamed. "You dumb, old Buzzard!"

"At least I wasn't dumb enough to let Rabbit saddle me up and ride me to town!" Buzzard shouted back.

That was the wrong thing to say, for Fox grabbed Buzzard by the tail and shook him till his feathers flew. "I can cut your head off with the ax," yelled Fox, "or I can throw you into the fire! You decide, Buzzard, which will it be?"

"Not the fire! Not the fire!" cried Buzzard. "Cut off my head, if you have to, Fox. But I'm afraid of fire!"

That was all Fox needed to hear. With a nasty grin, he tossed Buzzard at the flames, screaming, "Then I'm turning you into cinders!"

Buzzard's feet simply cleared the flames. He just stretched his big black wings and flapped calmly back up to his perch. "I'm also not so dumb," he laughed, "to forget that birds can fly!"